An ABC of what

When I'm Bigger

For Isla and Jaxon

Auctioneer   Acrobat

Actor

Architect

Astronaut

Aa

Art Director

Accountant

Artist

Animal Breeder   Analyst

Assistant   Audiologist

Aircraft Mechanic

Astronaut

Astronaut, Astronaut,
way up high.
Rockets shooting,
through the sky.

Bb

Beautician

Baker

Blacksmith

Bookeeper

Basketball Player

Builder

Bee keeper

Barrister

Banker

Babysitter

Bartender

Biochemist

Builder

Builders mixing,
dig, dig, dig.
Driving diggers,
small and big.

Chemist　　Chimney Sweep

Cake maker

Consultant

Constable

Cashier

Cc

Candlemaker

Cardiologist

Carpenter

Cleaner

Clown

Choreographer　Carpet Fitter

Circus Acrobat

Clown

Clowns smile.
Clowns frown.
Juggling balls,
Spinning around.

Driver

Dinosaur Explorer

Diver

Dermatologist

Dentist

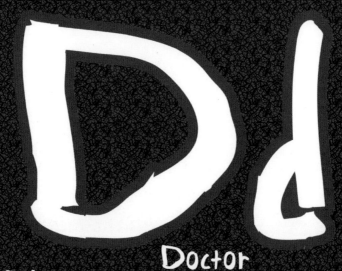

Doctor

Director

Decorator

Developer

Dancer

Dog Walker

Dog Trainer

Data Entry Clark

Daddy

Dancer

Hip hop, Ballet,
Foxtrot, Jive.
Counting the beat,
one-to-five.

Engraver

Explorer

Elf

Editor

Electrician

Egg Collector

Elephant Trainer

Engineer

Examiner

Embroiderer

Entertainer

Environmental Officer

Searching up high,
searching down low.
Discovering all,
the new places to go.

Ff

Fashion Designer

Florist

Farmer

Film Producer

Firefighter

Fire Inspector

First Aider

Forester

Fisherman

Farm Worker

Furniture Designer

Florist

Bright blossom.
growing huge trees.
Planting flowers,
for the honey bee's.

Gardener

Glazier

Geologist   Guard   Glass Cutter

Golfer

Gg

Gas Inspector

Ground Layer

Giraffe Walker

Guide   General Helper

Garbage Collector

Golfer

18 hole golf,
can be great fun.
Line it up,
get a hole in one.

Hh

Hat Designer

Head Teacher

Hotel Manager

Horse Trainer

Horse Rider

Hairdresser

Historian

Housekeeper

Health Officer

Hostess

Hypnotherapist

Hairdresser

Brushing, chopping,
snip, snip, snip.
Putting hair up,
using pretty clips.

Inspector

Instructor

Igloo Builder

IT Technician

Illustrator

Ironmonger

Ice Skater

Ice Cream Chef

Industrial Engineer

Instrument Repairer

Installer

Interior Designer

Inspector

Inspectors look out,
for naugty faces.
Solving crimes,
and all the tricky cases.

Jouster

Jockey

Joker

Judge

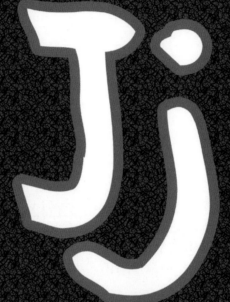

Jam Maker

Jewellery Designer

Joiner

Jigsaw Puzzle Designer

Judge

Good people, bad people,
liars and thugs.
To prison or not,
is the job of a Judge.

Koala Cuddler

Key Cutter

King

Kitchen Assistant

Kite Tester

Knitter

Kitten Breeder

Keyboard Musician

Karate Instructor

King

Waving to crowds.
It's fun to be King.
Looking after the Kingdom.
protecting everything.

Lifeguard

Lion Tamer

Lighting Engineer

Laundry Worker

Landscaper

Leaflet Distributor

Lawyer

Labourer

Librarian

Locksmith

Lifeguard

Sandcastles, sea,
waves and fun.
Helping people stay safe,
in water and sun.

Mm

Mummy

Mathematician

Manager

Machine Worker

Mechanic

Map Maker

Make-up Artist

Marine Engineer

Mail Clerk

Monkey Handler

Musician

Mummy

Shopping, school runs,
kisses and cuddles.
Story time, fun,
and jumping in puddles.

Nurse

Narrator

Neurologist

News Reader

Nanny

Nutritionist

Nail Artist

Necklace Designer

Network Manager

Nurse

Fixing cuts,
giving people jabs.
Helping people feel.
less poorly and sad.

Opera Singer

Optician

Operator

Office Worker

Organiser

Oo

Oil Rig Worker

Oven Cleaner

Origami Creator

Opthalmologist

Odd Job Man

Opera Singer

Powerful noises,
telling stories with song.
Filling ears with music,
voices so strong.

Paleontologist

Paramedic

Pharmacist

Personal Trainer

Plumber

Porter

P P

President

Psychologist

Post Office Worker

Pest Control Technician

Police Officer

Pathologist

Police Officer

Police Officer, Police Officer,
stopping speeding cars.
Catching naughty people,
putting them behind bars.

Quality Controller

Queen

Quiz Master

Quiet Librarian

Quilt Designer

Quad Bike Rider

Quartz Miner

Quarantine Officer

Queen

Running the country,
looking after the nation.
Head of the country,
a great inspiration.

Rigger

Receptionist

Roofer

Road Worker

Radiologist

Rr

Railway Worker

Rubbish Collector

Retail Manager

Racing Driver

Researcher

Robot Designer

Racing Driver

Changing tyres,
making cars safe.
Speeding and zooming,
winning the race.

Sailor

Sales Manager

Sound Technician

Surgeon

Signwriter

Ss

Scientist

Scaffolder

Solicitor

Sonographer

Sports Coach

Soldier

Social Worker

Safety Engineer

Ship's Captain

Soldier

March, Salute,
Left, right, left.
March, Salute,
Left, right, left.

Technical Officer

Tour Guide

Tree Surgeon

Tailor

T t

Teacher

Taxi Driver

Telephone Operator

Town Planner

Textile Designer

Tool Maker

Truck Driver

Train Driver

Tennis Player

Hitting the tennis ball,
over the net.
Scoring points,
winning the set.

Ultimate Party Planner

Umpire

Underwear Designer

Upholsterer

Uu

Usher

Underwriter

Unicorn Trainer

Unicycle Rider

Umbrella Creator

Ultra sound Technician

University Lecturer

Underwater Diver

Unicorn Trainer

Training Unicorns
to fly through hoops.
Up and down,
doing loop the loop.

Visual Merchandiser

Vicar

Vet

Van Driver

Vv

Vocal Trainer

Vice President

Volleyball Coach

Violin Player

Video Editor

Valet

Vegetable Picker

Vet

Rabbits, Guinea Pigs.
Cats and Dogs.
Fixing everything,
from Horses to Frogs.

Wizard

Warden

Wallpaper Decorator

Waitress

Waste Collector

Waiter

Water Surfer

Waltz Dancer

Water Polo Player

Waiter

Knives, forks,
spoons and food.
Hoping customers,
won't be rude.

X–Ray Technician

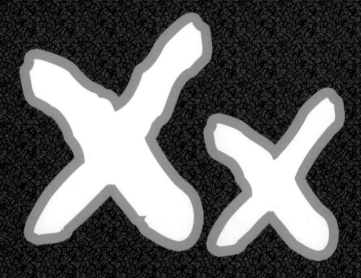

Xylophone Musician

X–Ray Fisherman

X-ray Technician

If you have a
super nasty fall,
an X-ray will find breaks,
big or small.

Yy

Yoga Teacher

Yacht Sailor

Youth Worker

Yard Manager

Yo-yo Artist

YouTuber

Yoghurt Flavour Designer

Yoga Teacher

Stretch up, stretch down,
touch the ground.
Spinning, sitting,
turning around and around.

Zoo Vet

Zebra Keeper

Zombie

Zz

Zip Maker

Zillionaire

Zen Garden Designer

Zoo Veterinarian

Zoo Keeper

Cleaning the Giraffes,
feeding the bears.

What will you be
when you are bigger?

You can be ANYTHING!!